亲爱的爸爸妈妈们：

在阅读这本书之前，您可以让您的孩子先在左侧的横线上写下自己的名字——这可能成为他（她）完完整整读完的第一本书，也因此成为真正意义上第一本属于他（她）自己的书。

作为美国最知名的儿童启蒙阅读丛书"I Can Read！"中的一册，它专为刚开始阅读起步的孩子量身打造，具有用词简单、句子简短、适当重复，以及注重语言的韵律和节奏等特点。这些特点非常有助于孩子对语言的学习，不论是学习母语，还是学习作为第二语言的英语。

故事的主角是鼎鼎大名的贝贝熊一家，这一风靡美国近半个世纪的形象对孩子具有天然的亲和力，很多跟贝贝熊有关的故事都为孩子所津津乐道。作为双语读物，它不但能引导孩子独立捧起书本，去了解书中有趣的情节，还能做到真正从兴趣出发，让孩子领略到英语学习的乐趣。

就从贝贝熊开始，让您的孩子爱上阅读，帮助他们开启自己的双语阅读之旅吧！

图书在版编目（CIP）数据

　　海滩挖宝记：汉英对照 / (美) 博丹 (Berenstain,J.)，(美) 博丹 (Berenstain,M.)
著；姚雁青译. —乌鲁木齐：新疆青少年出版社，2013.1
　　（贝贝熊系列丛书）
　　ISBN 978-7-5515-2739-2

　　Ⅰ. ①海… Ⅱ. ①博… ②博… ③姚… Ⅲ. ①英语－汉语－对照读物②儿童故
事－美国－现代 Ⅳ.①H319.4：I
　　中国版本图书馆CIP数据核字(2012)第273205号

版权登记：图字 29-2012-24

The Berenstain Bears' Seashore Treasure
copyright©2005 by Berenstain Bears, Inc.
This edition arranged with Sterling Lord Literistic, Inc.
through Andrew Nurnberg Associates International Limited

贝贝熊系列丛书
海滩挖宝记

(美) 斯坦·博丹　简·博丹　绘著　Stan & Jan Berenstain　　姚雁青　译

出 版 人　徐　江		策　划　许国萍	
责任编辑　贺艳华		美术编辑　查　璇　刘小珍	
法律顾问　钟　麟　13201203567（新疆国法律师事务所）			

新疆青少年出版社
（地址：乌鲁木齐市北京北路29号　邮编：830012）
Http://www.qingshao.net　　E-mail：QSbeijing@hotmail.com

印　　刷　北京时尚印佳彩色印刷有限公司		经　销　全国新华书店	
开　　本　787mm×1092mm　1/16		印　张　2	
版　　次　2013年1月第1版		印　次　2013年1月第1次印刷	
印　　数　1-1 0000册		定　价　9.00元	
标准书号　ISBN 978-7-5515-2739-2			

制售盗版必究 举报查实奖励:0991-7833932　版权保护办公室举报电话：0991-7833927
销售热线:010-84853493 84851485　　如有印刷装订质量问题 印刷厂负责掉换

The Berenstain Bears'
I Can Read!

贝贝熊系列丛书
双语阅读

SEASHORE TREASURE
海滩挖宝记

(美) 斯坦·博丹　简·博丹　绘著
Stan & Jan Berenstain

姚雁青　译

CHISO SINCE 1956　新疆青少年出版社

The Bear family was going to the seashore.
They were going across a bridge.

贝贝熊一家要去海边度假，
他们的车开上了一座大桥。

The bridge went to Laughing Gull Island.
It was called Laughing Gull Island
because so many laughing gulls lived there.
"*Ha! Ha! Ha!*" cried the laughing gulls
as they sailed across the sky.

这座大桥通往笑鸥岛。

有许许多多的笑鸥在这个岛上栖息，所以它被称作"笑鸥岛"。

"哈！哈！哈！"笑鸥们一边在空中翱翔，一边大叫。

"Will we be there soon?" asked Sister Bear.

"Yes," said Papa Bear.

"Do you see that house on the beach?
That is where we are going to stay."

"我们快到了吗？"小熊妹妹问。

"是的。看到海滩上的小屋了吗？"熊爸爸回答，

"那就是我们要住的地方。"

The Bear family unpacked the car.
They carried their things into the house.

贝贝熊一家从车上取下行李，扛着行李进了屋。

Brother, Sister, and Papa Bear
put on their swimsuits.
Mama decided to wait until later.
"Come, Papa," said Brother.
"Let's go to the beach."

小熊哥哥、小熊妹妹和熊爸爸换上了游泳衣。
熊妈妈打算过一会儿再换。
"爸爸，我们赶紧去海边吧！"小熊哥哥催促道。

"Hmm," said Papa.

"I found something in the closet."

"What is it?" asked Brother.

"It is a map," said Papa.

"An old pirate treasure map."

"等等，"熊爸爸说，"我在柜子里找到一样东西。"

"是什么呢？"小熊哥哥问。

"是张地图，一张古老的海盗藏宝图。"熊爸爸回答。

"Really, my dear," said Mama.

"It says this place used to be called Pirates Cove!" said Papa.

"It says that pirates buried their booty here."

"What is booty, Papa?" asked Sister.

"亲爱的，是真的吗？"熊妈妈吃惊地问。

"地图上说，这个地方曾经叫'海盗湾'！"熊爸爸说，

"这上面还说，海盗们把他们的战利品都埋在这里了。"

"爸爸，什么是战利品？"小熊妹妹问。

"It is treasure," said Papa.
"Pirate treasure. You know—gold, silver,
diamonds, and rubies."
"Now, really, my dear," said Mama.

"就是海盗抢来的财宝——金子、银子、钻石，还有红宝石什么的，
这叫作海盗的宝藏。"熊爸爸回答。
"哎哟，亲爱的，是真的吗？"熊妈妈吃惊地问。

"Do you think the map is real?"
asked Brother.
"There's only one way to find out,"
said Papa. "Follow me."

"您觉得这张藏宝图是真的吗？"小熊哥哥问。
"只有一个办法能知道答案，"熊爸爸说，"跟我来！"

Papa got a shovel.
They went down to the beach.

熊爸爸找来一把铁锹。然后，他们一起走向海滩。

It was a bright sunny day.

The sea sparkled.

Waves crashed upon the shore.

"*Ha! Ha! Ha!*" cried the laughing gulls.

这一天阳光灿烂。

海面上波光粼粼。

海浪冲刷着海岸。

"哈！哈！哈！"笑鸥们在空中不停地大叫。

Papa began to dig.
The cubs splashed in the sea.

熊爸爸开始挖坑。
小熊们在海水里跳跃嬉戏，溅起许多水花。

"Have you found any treasure yet, Papa?"
asked Brother.
"Not so far," said Papa.
"All I have found are some old shells."

"爸爸，您找到宝藏了吗？" 小熊哥哥问。
"还没有呢，" 熊爸爸回答，"我只挖到了一些老贝壳。"

"What is this one, Papa?"
asked Sister.
"That is a clam shell," said Papa.
"It is big and gray," said Sister.

"这是什么呀，爸爸？" 小熊妹妹问。
"这是一个蚌壳。" 熊爸爸回答。
"它好大呀，是灰色的。" 小熊妹妹说。

"What is this one?"
asked Brother.
"That is an oyster shell,"
said Papa.
"It is bumpy and black,"
said Brother.

"这是什么呀？" 小熊哥哥问。
"这是一个牡蛎壳。" 熊爸爸回答。
"它好粗糙呀，是黑色的。" 小熊哥哥说。

Papa looked at the treasure map.

"Hmm," he said.

"This must not be the right spot."

熊爸爸仔细看了看藏宝图，然后说：
"嗯，这里肯定不是藏宝的地方。"

He moved to another spot
and dug some more.

他换了一个地方，又挖了好多坑。

"Any treasure yet, Papa?"
asked Brother.
"No, just more old shells," said Papa.

"找到宝藏了吗，爸爸？"小熊哥哥问。
"没有，只挖到了更多的老贝壳。"熊爸爸回答。

"What is this one?"
asked Brother.
"That is a scallop shell,"
said Papa.
"It is pretty and pink,"
said Sister.

"这是什么呀？"小熊哥哥问。
"这是一个扇贝壳。"熊爸爸回答。
"它好漂亮，是粉色的呢。"小熊妹妹赞叹道。

"What are shells for?" asked Brother.
"Shells are the homes
of some sea animals," said Papa.
"The clam shell was the home of a clam.
The oyster shell was the home of an oyster.
The scallop shell was the home of a scallop."

"这些贝壳有什么用啊?" 小熊哥哥问。
"它们是一些海洋动物的家。"熊爸爸回答,
"蚌壳是蚌的家。牡蛎壳是牡蛎的家。扇贝壳是扇贝的家。"

The sun shone down.

The sea sparkled.

Waves crashed upon the shore.

"*Ha! Ha! Ha!*" cried the laughing gulls.

太阳照在海面上。

海水烁烁闪亮。

海浪冲刷着海岸。

"哈！哈！哈！"笑鸥们在空中不停地大叫。

"Papa, what happened to the clam,
the oyster, and the scallop?" asked Sister.

"爸爸，那些蚌、牡蛎，还有扇贝上哪儿去了呢？"
小熊妹妹问。

"I guess maybe the laughing gulls
got them," said Papa.
Papa looked at the map again.
"Hmm," he said.
"This must not be the right spot."

"我猜它们都被笑鸥吃掉了吧。"熊爸爸回答。
熊爸爸又看了看地图。
"嗯，这里肯定不是藏宝的地方。"他说。

He went to another spot and dug some more.

"Any treasure yet, Papa?" asked Sister.

"I'm afraid not," said Papa.

"Just some more old shells."

熊爸爸又走到另一个地方，挖了更多的坑。

"挖到宝藏了吗，爸爸？" 小熊妹妹问。

"恐怕还没有，" 熊爸爸回答，"只挖到了更多的老贝壳。"

"You know something?" said Papa.
"Digging for treasure is hot work!"
"*Ha! Ha! Ha!*" cried the laughing gulls.
"Hmm," said Papa.
"Do you think those gulls are laughing at us
and our treasure hunt?"

"你们知道吗？"熊爸爸说，"挖宝藏让我流了好多汗呢！"
"哈！哈！哈！"笑鸥们在空中不停地大叫。
"嗯，你们觉得这些海鸥是在笑话我们吗？
它们是不是在笑我们的寻宝行动？"熊爸爸问小熊们。

"No way!" said Brother.
"We came looking for treasure
and we found it.
We found *the treasure of the sea*!"
"That's right," said Sister.
"A whole bucket full!"

"才不是呢！"小熊哥哥大声说，
"我们来这里寻宝，还真的找到了宝藏。
我们找到了大海的宝藏！"
"是啊，满满一大桶呢！"小熊妹妹也嚷道。

"Time for a dip!" said Papa.

"我们去泡海水澡吧！" 熊爸爸提议。

After they cooled off
they headed back to the house
to show Mama their treasure.

等凉快够了，
他们一起回屋，
给熊妈妈看他们找到的宝藏。

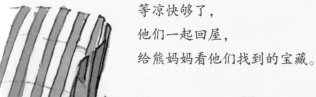

"Papa," said Brother, "what are you going to do with the treasure map?"
"Hmm," said Papa, "I may just leave it in the closet for the next papa bear."

"爸爸," 小熊哥哥问, "那张藏宝图怎么办?"
"呵呵," 熊爸爸说, "我要把它放回柜子, 让下一位来这儿度假的熊爸爸也去寻寻宝。"